TOKIWA; A JAPANESE LOVE STORY

Tokiwa; A Japanese Love Story
ISBN-13: 978-1-937981-59-4

Authors: Kambiz Mostofizadeh & Onoto Watana

Publisher: Mikazuki Publishing House
www.MikazukiPublishingHouse.com

The information contained within this book is for

educational and commercial purposes and does not

necessarily reflect the views of the publisher.

1

TOKIWA: A JAPANESE LOVE STORY

For fourteen consecutive days she

had remained before the shrine, eating no

food, drinking little water, sleeping not.

Mechanically she went through the

monotonous motions, bending her body

back and forth, until it seemed like some

mechanical puppet, working clock-like back

and forth, her parched, weary lips uttering

only the feeble common prayer of the

devout Buddhist:

Namu, Amida Butsu!" ("Save us, Eternal

Buddha!")

A venerable bonze, almost blind and

entirely bald, slipped his rosary drowsily

from finger to finger. Tokiwa saw him not,

though well she knew that he was at her

side, and ever her dry lips intoned: *"Namu,*

Amida Butsu!" Thus, for fourteen days.

Then she dropped forward, her brow

striking for the last time the stone feet of the

great image.

The bonze, assured of the completeness of

her penance, carried her aloft into the great

hall of the nuns. There he left her, in peace

at last, and started upon his pilgrimage.

Many years before, hundreds of

3

TOKIWA; A JAPANESE LOVE STORY

monks had congregated before this same,

then-gorgeous, altar, chanting their

splendid ritual; but the fanatical Nichiren

sect had pointed out to the world the

faithlessness of its priests—who ate the

forbidden meat, who lived in open

luxury and licentiousness, who flaunted

their wealth in the face of a poverty-bowed

world, and whose political power knew no

limit. A zealous band of bigots of this rival

sect attempted to burn the monastery. It

had withstood the assault of the

incendiaries, but the marks and ravages of

the attack were physically upon its walls. It

became uninhabitable for monks of wealth

and ambition. For years it remained

untenanted, a weird yet rugged old mass,

stripped of its wealth, but not its beauty—

deserted, falling to the decay of neglected

age.

A bonze at the Court of the Emperor,

an eager missionary and loyal servant,

incurred the displeasure of the Emperor's

master, the Shogun, or warlord of Japan.

Without warning his family had been

5

attacked and practically exterminated.

Driven from pillar to post, he found himself

at last a deserted fugitive, with nothing

remaining to him but the dear one at his

feet, she who had followed him upon all his

wanderings. In the act of committing

seppuku, he perceived the wide, appealing

glance of the child upon her back. It too, still

lived. Swiftly the sword was replaced, and

he set himself another task. He penned a

humble petition to his enemy, finding in a

fisherman a willing courier to the capital.

His request was granted. He was ordered

TOKIWA; A JAPANESE LOVE STORY

to shave his head and retire to the ruined

monastery on the shore of Kamakura.

In this retreat, the broken-spirited

bonze gave himself up to a life of prayer

and piety. Here the child, Tokiwa, grew to

girlhood in solitude and innocence. From

the first she had been given by her

grandfather as a sacrificial offering for his

sins to the Lord Buddha. She knew no

speech save that couched in the language

of prayer and admonition. To her, life meant

one constant act of expiation, of prayer,

fasting, for mortal sin committed in

TOKIWA: A JAPANESE LOVE STORY

some former state. She accepted her lot

piously, humbly, sweetly. Only sometimes

she could not forbear running out into the

sunlight, to smile at the blue skies above

her, to stretch out her hands to the stars, to

whisper back to the golden fields which

spread out beyond their overgrown

temple gardens.

Not even the people from the

nearest village visited the deserted temple,

save when rare pilgrimages were made to

the place; and then they who went told, with

shudders, of the unspeakably old, blind

TOKIWA; A JAPANESE LOVE STORY

bonze at the shrine, and the weird sprite

face of the child nun, who danced alone in

the deserted temple, to please the deities.

It was summer. The bees had made

a hive in one of the out-jutting eaves of the

temple. The world was saffron colored, the

hills, the skies, the fields, dim purple. A

traveler pushed his way through the tangled

brushwood, and paused before the ruined

temple. He stood like one lost in the

meshes of a strange dream. So deserted

and still seemed this refuge he had sought

that at first he wondered dazedly whether

9

indeed there was life within.

Then he saw the sliding of the

window screen, and Tokiwa leaned far out.

She reached up a slim bamboo rod, poked

at the eave and dislodged the hive. A

moment of retreat from the angry bees, and

then she cautiously slipped the *shoji* open

again and obtained the coveted honey.

Within arm's length of the sacred shrine,

she crouched upon her heels, eating the

sweet morsel she had stolen.

A sunbeam came through an

opening door and fell like a searchlight

upon her little startled face. She thought of

the reverend bonze, remembered her

devotions, and thinking now only of her

sins, fell upon her knees, putting her face

upon the floor. A strange voice spoke her

name, very gently, and she looked up

slowly.

"Art thou Tokiwa?"

When she had recovered from her

human amazement, she answered that she

was indeed, miserably, that sinful and guilty

worm, Tokiwa, grandchild of the temple

bonze. Then, human feelings again

TOKIWA: A JAPANESE LOVE STORY

assailing her, she asked: "And thou?"

To which replied the boy, with a smile

strangely sad: "Like yourself, a poor exile

and fugitive, seeking an asylum from

Shinran, the bonze, once my august

father's friend and servant."

Now Tokiwa knew nothing of the

history of the times. She knew little indeed

of her own history, save that in some former

state she had sinned grievously, hence her

expiation in this present life. Of the state of

unrest and oppression, of civil war, of

intriguing factions, of intolerable humiliation

TOKIWA: A JAPANESE LOVE STORY

of the Mikado's, she had heard never the

faintest murmur. To her, the Mikado was a

deity, the chief of all indeed, for this the

bonze had taught her, clinging still to the

Shinto belief despite his Buddhism. In the

tangled reasoning of the child mind of

Tokiwa, the world without was very good

and beautiful. People there were joyful; they

did not need to suffer for their sins. The

deities were not punishing them. Penance

was reserved for such benighted ones as

she. Now here, apparently, stood before

her another sinner like herself, one who

TOKIWA; A JAPANESE LOVE STORY

said he too had been driven into exile. They

were kindred spirits, twins in suffering. She

went toward him slowly, wide-eyed, her

cheeks and lips red as the poppies tossed

at the feet of the great Buddha, for Tokiwa

was too poor to make a richer offering.

With small hands crossed upon her bosom,

like some fascinated creature, she stood in

silence, looking at him, very near to him, so

near indeed, that he inhaled the breath of

the incense in her garments, the subtle

odor of *umegaku* and the pine. It clung

about her, upon her garments, in her hair,

14

her very body. Her eyes were like liquid pools of dense blackness into which his own seemed to have leaped and lost their soul. "Tokiwa!" he whispered lowly, and now he reached and touched the little crossed hands upon her bosom. They did not unclasp, but they trembled under the warm touch of his hand.

She began upon her prayers, but her voice caught upon the words. She could not finish them. Never in her life before had a human hand held her own; never had she looked into the eyes of a fellow mortal. The

TOKIWA: A JAPANESE LOVE STORY

stone gaze of the Buddhas was calm, with

a wisdom past understanding, but never

they smiled, and always the touch of their

feet, where daily she put her small meek

head, was cold.

Unconsciously her own lips and eyes

caught the infection of the boy's smiling

gaze, and, as she smiled, again he

spoke:

"Tokiwa, how beautiful thou art. Pray you,

smile again!" Some vague feeling of unrest

stirred within her. She clutched her heart

tightly, as if to stay its tumultuous

TOKIWA: A JAPANESE LOVE STORY

beating. "Hush!" she whispered, "Buddha

will hear!" He followed her, catching at her

fluttering sleeve, as, soundlessly, she fled

across the great room of worship and

disappeared into an interior apartment.

He was seventeen, a youth born and bred

in the refined, lavish luxury of the imperial

court. It had been customary for the

Shogun to raise its Mikado in this

effeminate form, making him merely a child

in intelligence and hence a figurehead in

authority. His features were delicate, his

arched eyebrows as sensitive as a poet's,

his lips as full and pouting as a child's. He

had a tender chin and brow. His eyes were

large and long, and somewhat melancholy,

but there were latent hints within them of a

stronger power possible of awakening. He

was slim of figure and exquisite in his

bearing. He moved indolently, but with

grace. From day to day he wandered about

the dusty, silent temple, bowing

mechanically before its effigies, examining

the wonderful art work indelibly printed

upon its walls, going about from room to

room, climbing up and down its eight

18

TOKIWA: A JAPANESE LOVE STORY

stories, and always eternally seeking,

seeking, seeking.

But no longer Tokiwa danced for the

deities; no longer her graceful little body

prostrated itself before the shrine. No

longer she touched the great foot of the

stone Buddha with her small meek brow.

The wind-bells tinkled. A hummingbird flew

under its glass. Under the sun the lotus in

the unmoving water opened their white

fingers, revealing the golden heart within. A

hand, white as the lotus itself, pushed its

flat-shaped leaves aside and over the clear

19

mirror of the water thus revealed, a girl's eager face looked and looked.

What instinct had guided her to the pool? How could she know the water alone in all this deserted wilderness would show her, her beauty? Maybe at some time before the coming of Prince Go-Yoshi she had dreamily watched the slim outline of her small, reflected hand upon the water and thus had learned of nature's mirror.

However it be, for seven days she had obeyed the injunction of the reverend bonze. She had performed her devotions in

TOKIWA; A JAPANESE LOVE STORY

another part of the temple, mindful that it

would be unseemly for one so humble to

appear before the Son of Heaven, for such,

she was assured, their visitor would

someday be, or mayhap was already. And

so to him she intoned her perpetual

prayers. Of him she had dreamed, and

waking, dreamed again. Unconsciously the

words he had spoken came to her lips:

"Tokiwa! How beautiful thou art! Pray you,

smile again."

Now, in the dawn, she had come to

the pool, irresistibly drawn there by the

eternal feminine within her, to prove

him.

As she looked, whispering

mechanically the recurring words of her

prayer, she saw that other face coming

beside her own, there in the water beneath.

For a moment she did not stir. Then as he

spoke her name, his lips almost touching

the small pink shell of her ear, she turned

to him throbbingly:

"Anata!" (Thou at last!)

"Where hast thou been, beloved?" A caress

was upon every word he spoke.

"I have been praying," she faltered.

"For what?" he asked.

"My sins," she said.

At that he smiled.

"*Your* sins, Tokiwa?"

She caught her breath as if she could not

find the words she wished "for I am not like

you, exalted one!" Suddenly she

remembered to whom she spoke, and

slipping down tremulously from the wall of

the pool, she put her head at his feet,

beginning her wistful prayer:

"*Namu, Amida—*"

TOKIWA: A JAPANESE LOVE STORY

Stooping, he lifted her to her feet. She

found herself held in the curve of his arm,

his cheek against her own.

They spoke not at all, only moving step by

step, about the old, overgrown temple

gardens. Summer had left only its last

touches of deep bronze upon the land.

Earth was sighing with its too swift

departure. Already the trees had begun to

drop their glorified freight. Like our best

hopes which elude us, they slipped one by

one from the branches, leaving them bare,

hungry, naked! But still the nightingale

TOKIWA: A JAPANESE LOVE STORY

poured forth its passionate heart to

the starlit nights. "Listen," said the Prince

Go-Yoshi, "I will tell you my dream

of last night. Once, many moons ago, in the

season of White Dew, you and I met and

loved. You were a white butterfly drowsing

on the heart of a wild poppy. I was *agaki*—a

thing of evil! I had the form of a scorpion,

and always I wandered restlessly about,

seeking prey for my death sting. I saw you

asleep on the heart of the poppy, and

slipping up behind, I found my way, bent

upon your destruction. Suddenly you

fluttered your white wings upward, and

then in my dream, Tokiwa—I saw your

eyes, just as they are now, beloved, and all

the evil dropped away from my heart. I was

no longer a *gaki*; but a palpitating

repentant, pleading with the Lord Buddha to

make me worthy of your touch. As am I

now, dear beloved!"

She shivered slightly, and he slipped his

arm out of the sleeve of his *haori* and drew

half of it about her. Her voice was timid.

She had the accent of one speaking a new

language. "The Son of Heaven cannot sin!"

26

TOKIWA: A JAPANESE LOVE STORY

"Nay, beloved. The deities belong not to

Earth. Not even the Mikado's are divine.

Nor I. I am like you, Tokiwa, human-deities

only when transported by our love. Yet

hear me swear, as we stand beneath the

open heavens, where we are told blessed

Nirvana may sometime be found: for the

time of this life, and as many after as may

come, I will be your husband and take you

for my wife.

Make me the same promise, beloved."

Her lips could not frame the words, her

eyes speaking the language he longed to

hear. Suddenly a cloud passed over

her face. She pushed herself free, holding

him back with her hands upon his breast.

"When they shall come for you!" she said.

"Tokiwa!"

"Thou hast told me of your father's wrongs,

and Oh! The sufferings of your people!"

The old blind bonze came tottering toward

them, feeling his way with his staff,

knocking upon the bare tree trunks, the

now leafless shrubs.

"Son of Heaven!" he cried, his voice gaining

a strange power from the emotion deep-seated within him, "The time has come at

last!"

He put the dispatch brought by a

courier into the boy's trembling hand. It

slipped from his nerveless fingers ere he

could read it, and fell fluttering to the

ground. An aimless wind caught the wisp

of paper and blew it against the *obi* of

Tokiwa. There it rested, against her heart.

Her band closed upon it with a sudden

strength. She thrust it into the boy's

tightly clenched fist.

"Go!" she throbbingly whispered. "Your

TOKIWA: A JAPANESE LOVE STORY

father calls you.

Your people need you!"

Suddenly the ancient bonze intoned

solemnly the warrior's prayer to Hachiman,

the deity of War.

"Namu, Hachiman, Dai Bosatsu!"

("Glory to Hachiman, the Incarnation of

Buddha!")

The Prince Go-Yoshi caught his breath in a

sobbing gasp. But he had turned about at

last. He did not look back. Always the

parent comes first. Duty is higher than love.

Thus from the suffocating struggle of heart

TOKIWA: A JAPANESE LOVE STORY

and mind Go-Yoshi emerged noble. Tokiwa

was ejected, not from the heart, but from

the mind, which at this time could hold but

one mighty impulse. These were the

troublesome times of the Hojo Clan rule

and for the first time in the history of Japan,

the Emperor's condition was so deplorable,

that often he knew not the bodily comfort of

an ordinary citizen. At the cruel mercy of

the warlords, their condition was pitiable.

One boy emperor was set up only to be

deposed for another, often his own infant

son. So rapid was the change from one boy

31

TOKIWA: A JAPANESE LOVE STORY

emperor to another, that princes of the true

blood and direct line were now nearly

exhausted. Yet this was the rule of Hojo

Clan. Infant sovereigns, divine figure-

heads in the eyes of the world! And the real

Mikado in exile! Now Go-Yoshi's turn had

come; but not as a puppet went the boy

back to the great capital. His father,

already banished to Oki, needed succor.

The Prince Go-Yoshi heeded the

impassioned promise of the gallant little

army which had rallied to his support. He

planned to assist his father to recover the

32

imperial power, and this at the price of his

own forfeit of the throne as a puppet of

Mikado. Not easily was the mighty power

of the Hojo Clan to be overthrown.   In the

delirium of defeat, there in the besieged

and burning fortress of Kasagi in Yamato

province, Prince Go-Yoshi gave himself up

to despair. A bonze, blind, tottering, so old

his trembling hands could barely support

his staff, made his staggering way into the

beleaguered fortress. With his head at the

feet of the Prince Go-Yoshi he brought

strange tidings, and a promised solution to

33

TOKIWA; A JAPANESE LOVE STORY

the dangers now besetting the youth.

The Hojo Clan were to be propitiated.

Where the road from Kamakura meets the

beach, a vision of extraordinary loveliness

entrances the beholder. Here the fairest of

all islands shows its face of eternal green.

The ocean tosses its waters upon

Enoshima's shore like a great, playful

mother, washing her best-loved child. In the

distance the mountains of Idzu are dimly

seen, and, as if enthroned as Queen of the

World, above all, Fujiyama raises her head

of snow. Along this road where nature

seemed to show only her gentlest

and kindest aspects, the hosts of Hojo

traveled.

Whither? There was no enemy to be

met and destroyed hereabouts. The lately

rebellious Mikados, father and son, were

subdued; the former sent, heels up in his

palanquin, disgraced into exile, there to die

of a broken heart. But for the latter, the

bonze had bought a pardon, purchasing it

at a curious price, another prince of the true

blood! Hands tied behind him, lest he do

himself injury, his eyes bound about with a

cloth, the Prince Go-Yoshi, upon his

knees in his palanquin, was carried under

guard of the soldiers of the Hojo Clan; for

as a hostage should he be held until the

bonze had redeemed his promise.

Suddenly the cortege halted. Seemingly in

the heart of the woods, it had come upon a

curious sight, one seen only near the

habitations of men. But here no dwelling,

no meanest hut, nor smallest cot, told of

human abode. Yet hidden only by the giant

pines, centuries old, a few *cho* from the

cortege, the ragged peaks of the old temple

of Kamakura seemed to fling up their

defiant ears skyward. Under the very

shadow of its gloom, someone had set up

the "flowing invocation!" Only a sheet of

cotton, suspended upon four sticks driven

into the ground! How eloquent its meaning!

How effective upon even the roughest, the

hardest-hearted of the warriors of the

bloodthirsty Hojo Clan.

One stooped to the little brook hard

by, and offering a prayer with the aid of his

rosary beads, poured the water over the

cloth, waiting patiently for it to strain

through, ere he passed the dipper to a

brother soldier. One by one, solemnly in

turn, they performed the charitable function.

How significant to them this simple sheet of

cotton! It told of mother love and mother

pain. Mutely it appealed to the passersby

for the love of all the deities, to shorten the

sufferings of one in agony. Thus the mother

who dies in childbirth, guilty of some awful

offense in a previous existence, or in this

life, must travel through the darkness

of the lowest Hades, until through the

compassion of the passers-by the cloth is

worn out by the water poured upon

it.

Here in the woods, far from the dwelling-place of men, who should there be to shorten the period of suffering of the child Tokiwa, mother of a new Emperor of Japan? Did not the fourteen days of penance at the altar, ere the coming of the child, suffice? The bonze undid the cloth which bound the prince's eyes, and set free the imprisoned hands. And still he did not move. His dazzled eyes saw not, or, if they did, heeded not, the "flowing invocation," and the reverent, silenced warriors about it.

Only they saw the grizzled walls of the

old Kamakura temple; and something

welled up and stirred within the frozen heart

of the poor defeated one, captive in the

hands of the dreaded Hojo. The bloody

days of soul torture, of physical suffering, of

fire, starvation, humiliation, and surrender,

all that had written their record in letters of

fire upon the mind of the Prince Go-Yoshi,

forgotten! A woman's face, nay, but a

child's, came back to his memory's eyes.

"Tokiwa!" he suddenly cried aloud,

dashing against the door of the temple, and

plunged into its deserted interior. There, in

the sunlight admitted by the opened door, a

moment he lingered, where little Tokiwa

had danced for the deities! He ran from

room to room, fleeing up the eight flights of

stairs, like one pursued rather than

pursuing. His voice vibrated with his

struggling emotions, now hopeful joy, now

fear, unknown:

"Tokiwa! Tokiwa! Tokiwa!"

And then at last:

"Oh, my beloved!"

TOKIWA; A JAPANESE LOVE STORY

He had come upon her in the great hall of

the nuns. Here where once hundreds of

maiden souls had rested from their prayers,

Tokiwa slept alone, her still pure and

innocent face thrown back upon the ooden

pillow, as if she looked upward at the faces

of the compassionate deities on the great

vaulted ceiling overhead.

THE END

TOKIWA: A JAPANESE LOVE STORY

NOTES

TOKIWA; A JAPANESE LOVE STORY

NOTES

TOKIWA: A JAPANESE LOVE STORY

NOTES

TOKIWA: A JAPANESE LOVE STORY

NOTES

TOKIWA: A JAPANESE LOVE STORY

NOTES

TOKIWA: A JAPANESE LOVE STORY

NOTES

TOKIWA: A JAPANESE LOVE STORY

NOTES

TOKIWA: A JAPANESE LOVE STORY

Mikazuki Publishing House is a proud

member of the Independent Book

Publishers Association

"EDUCATION IS THE KEY TO

HAPPINESS"

www.MikazukiPublishingHouse.com

www.ingramcontent.com/pod-product-compliance
Lightning Source LLC
Chambersburg PA
CBHW070609180626

46817CB00005B/2064